Franklin Plays Hockey

From an episode of the animated TV series *Franklin* produced by Nelvana Limited, Neurones France s.a.r.l. and Neurones Luxembourg S.A., based on the Franklin books by Paulette Bourgeois and Brenda Clark.

TV tie-in adaptation written by Sharon Jennings and illustrated by Mark Koren, John Lei and Jelena Sisic.

Based on the TV episode *Franklin Plays Hockey*, written by Brian Lasenby.

Franklin

Franklin is a trademark of Kids Can Press Ltd.
The character Franklin was created by Paulette Bourgeois and Brenda Clark.
Text © 2002 Contextx Inc.
Illustrations © 2002 Brenda Clark Illustrator Inc.

Kids Can Press acknowledges the financial support of the Ontario Arts Council, the Canada Council for the Arts and the Government of Canada, through the BPIDP, for our publishing activity.

Published in Canada by
Kids Can Press Ltd.
29 Birch Avenue
Toronto, ON M4V 1E2

Published in the U.S. by
Kids Can Press Ltd.
2250 Military Road
Tonawanda, NY 14150

www.kidscanpress.com

Edited by Tara Walker and Jennifer Stokes

Printed and bound in China
The hardcover edition of this book is smyth sewn casebound.
The paperback edition of this book is limp sewn with a drawn-on cover.

CM 02 0 9 8 7 6 5 4 3 2 1
CDN PA 02 0 9 8 7 6 5 4 3 2

National Library of Canada Cataloguing in Publication Data

Jennings, Sharon
    Franklin plays hockey / Sharon Jennings ; illustrated by Mark Koren, John Lei, Jelena Sisic.

(A Franklin TV storybook)
The character Franklin was created by Paulette Bourgeois and Brenda Clark.

ISBN 978-1-55337-056-7 (bound) ISBN 978-1-55337-057-4 (pbk.)

I. Bourgeois, Paulette II. Clark, Brenda III. Koren, Mark IV. Lei, John V. Sisic, Jelena VI. Title. VII. Series: Franklin TV storybook.

PS8569.E563F7185 2002   jC813'.54   C2002-901545-6
PZ7

Kids Can Press is a *corus*™ Entertainment company

Franklin Plays Hockey

Kids Can Press

FRANKLIN loved sports. In spring, summer and fall, he played baseball and soccer. In winter, he played hockey. As soon as the pond was frozen, Franklin was the first one to lace up his skates.

One cold winter day, Franklin hurried to the pond.
He was out on the ice by the time his friends arrived.
Bear put on his helmet and picked up his stick.
"Think we'll win today?" he asked.
"We always do," laughed Franklin.
Beaver scowled.

The game started. Within minutes, Franklin had scored the first two goals. It wasn't long before Bear scored, too.

"This is fun!" exclaimed Bear.

"Hmmph!" muttered Beaver. "It would be *fun* if my team was winning."

The friends raced up and down the pond. Franklin scored goals and blocked shots. After his fifth goal, he heard cheers from the hillside.

"Can Raccoon and I play, too?" called Skunk.

"Sure," answered Franklin. "Get your skates on and pick a team."

Skunk chose Franklin's team. Raccoon chose Beaver's.

"I'm not as good as you and Bear," Skunk warned.

"Don't worry," replied Franklin. "We're just having fun."

But soon, Franklin wasn't having much fun at all.
Skunk couldn't do anything right. She couldn't skate
fast, and she couldn't pass the puck. She couldn't
break up a play, and she couldn't shoot on net. When
Franklin got a breakaway, Skunk fell over and
knocked him down.

Then, Raccoon scored three goals, one right after
the other.

"*Now* I'm having fun!" declared Beaver.

When Raccoon scored another goal, Franklin
said it was time to quit.

"What's wrong, Franklin?" teased Beaver.
"Scared of losing?"

Franklin shrugged. "I'm just tired," he said.

"Then let's play again tomorrow morning," suggested Rabbit.

Franklin looked at Skunk.

"Uh ... same teams?" he asked.

"Of course!" said Beaver.

As everyone headed home, Skunk caught up
to Franklin.

"You'll have a better chance of winning
tomorrow without me," she said. "I'll come and
cheer for you, but I won't play."

"Oh, Skunk, I ...," Franklin started to say.

But Skunk had hurried off.

At dinner that night, Franklin picked at his food. He didn't finish even one piece of fly pie. When his parents asked what was wrong, Franklin told them about Skunk.

"I don't want to lose tomorrow's game," Franklin explained. "But I don't want Skunk to feel bad, either."

"It isn't easy being part of a team," said his father.

"I thought hockey was supposed to be fun," Franklin groaned.

In the morning, Franklin called on Bear.

"Skunk isn't going to play with us today," he told Bear. "She thinks she isn't good enough."

"But she's only played one game," Bear replied. "We had to play lots of games before we were any good."

"Remember when Jack Rabbit let us play with all the big kids?" Franklin asked.

Bear laughed. "I couldn't even stand up," he said.

Franklin sighed. "I wish we were still playing with Jack Rabbit," he said. "He'd know what to do."

When Franklin and Bear got to the pond, they saw Skunk. She was out on the ice, skating back and forth.

"Don't worry," called Skunk. "I'm not here to play. I'm just practising for next season."

"Next season?!" Franklin exclaimed.

"Maybe by then I'll be as good as you, Franklin," she said.

Franklin laughed. "I wasn't always this good," he said. "Once, I scored a goal on my own net."

"You did?" Skunk asked.

Franklin nodded. "I made lots of mistakes at first."

"You sure have gotten better," said Bear.

Franklin thought for a moment.

"I sure have," he said slowly.

Franklin watched as Skunk untied her skates. Suddenly, he knew what to do.

"Skunk, wait," he said. "If I got better the more I played, then so will you. You have to play with us."

"You mean you want me on your team one day?" asked Skunk.

"I mean I want you on my team *today*," answered Franklin.

Then he added, "Hockey is a *team* sport, Skunk. You can't get better practising all by yourself."

Skunk grinned. Then she bent down to tie up her skates.

Soon the other team arrived, and the game got started. Cheers and yells echoed around the ice. Franklin and Bear each scored a goal, but so did Beaver and Raccoon.

Then, Franklin got a breakaway. The empty net loomed ahead. No one was near him ... except Skunk.

"Stick on the ice!" Franklin called to Skunk.
A second later, he passed her the puck.
Skunk caught the pass. She wound up, shot ...
and scored.

Skunk whooped and hollered.
"I feel like a real hockey player!" she exclaimed.
"You are!" said Franklin. "And I feel like part of a team."